The Secret Garden

Frances Hodgson Burnett

Condensed and Adapted by
MARGARET DeKEYSER

Illustrated by
PHIL DEVINE

Cover Illustrated by
BILL MAUGHAN

Dalmatian Press

The Junior Classics have been
adapted and illustrated with care and thought
to introduce you to a world of famous authors, characters, ideas,
and great stories that have been loved for generations.

Editor — Kathryn Knight
Creative Director — Gina Rhodes-Haynes
And the entire classics project team
of Dalmatian Publishing Group

THE SECRET GARDEN

Printed in the United States of America

A note to the reader—

A classic story rests in your hands. The characters are famous. The tale is timeless.

This Junior Classic edition of *The Secret Garden* has been carefully condensed and adapted from the original version (which you really *must* read when you're ready for every detail). We kept the well-known phrases for you. We kept Frances Hodgson Burnett's style. And we kept the important imagery and heart of the tale.

Literature is terrific fun! It encourages you to think. It helps you dream. It is full of heroes and villains, suspense and humor, adventure and wonder, and new ideas. It introduces you to writers who reach out across time to say: "Do you want to hear a story I wrote?"

Curl up and enjoy.

CONTENTS

CHARACTERS

MARY LENNOX — an English child who lived in India until her parents died

THE AYAH — an Indian servant who took care of young Mary

MRS. LENNOX — Mary's mother, called Mem Sahib by the Indian servants out of respect

ENGLISH MINISTER — he and his family of five children keep Mary just after the death of her parents

BASIL — the mean son of the English minister

MR. ARCHIBALD CRAVEN — Mary's uncle, who takes Mary in to live with him at his home, Misselthwaite Manor, in Yorkshire, England

MRS. MEDLOCK — Mr. Craven's strict housekeeper who likes to keep order

MR. PITCHER — Mr. Craven's elderly personal servant

CHARACTERS

MARTHA SOWERBY — a young housemaid at Misselthwaite Manor and friend to Mary

DICKON SOWERBY — Martha's twelve-year-old brother, who is a nature lover

MOTHER (Susan Sowerby) — Martha's and Dickon's mother

BEN WEATHERSTAFF — an elderly gardener at Misselthwaite Manor

COLIN — Mr. Craven's sickly, spoiled, and lonely son

DR. CRAVEN — Colin's doctor and uncle

ROBIN, CAPTAIN, SOOT, NUT, SHELL, AND JUMP — Dickon's bird and animal friends

THE NURSE — Colin's nurse

The Secret Garden

CHAPTER ONE

There Is No One Left

Mary Lennox was a sour-looking child. She was very thin and always sick. Her skin was yellowish and her blonde hair was scraggly. Her father was an officer for the English Government in India. He was busy with his work so he didn't have time for Mary. Her mother was a great beauty who loved to go to parties and have fun. She didn't want a child at all. So Mary was handed over to an Ayah, a native servant. Mary's mother told the Ayah to keep the child out of her sight as much as possible.

Mary could only remember being cared for by her Ayah and the other native servants. They always let her have her own way. They knew that

Mrs. Lennox, or the Mem Sahib as they called her, would be angry if she was bothered by Mary's crying. Poor Mary was as spoiled as a little pig by the time she was six.

One very hot morning, she woke up feeling crabby. She became crabbier still when she saw that the servant in her room was not her Ayah. She was not very nice to Ayah, but she did not want anyone else to take care of her.

"Why did you come?" she said to the strange woman. "Send my Ayah to me."

The woman looked scared and told Mary that the Ayah could not come. Mary threw a fit. Even though Mary kicked her, the servant told her again that the Ayah could not come.

There was something strange happening at the Lennox house that morning. Everyone hurried around. Nothing was done on schedule. The servants acted scared and some of them seemed to be missing. No one would tell Mary anything. She was left alone as the morning went on.

Later, Mary was playing in a corner of the veranda. She saw her mother talking with a young British officer whom Mary didn't know. Mary usually called her mother Mem Sahib like the servants did, not Mama or Mother. Mary stared at her mother because she did not get to see her very often. The Mem Sahib was tall, slim, and very pretty. Her hair was like curly silk and

she wore the prettiest lacy clothes. But today the Mem Sahib looked scared.

"Is it very bad? Oh, is it?" Mary heard her ask.

"It's awful, Mrs. Lennox," the officer answered. "You should have left the city two weeks ago."

"Oh, I know," cried the Mem Sahib. "I only stayed to go to that silly dinner party. What a fool I was!"

Then a terrible wailing came from inside the house.

"What is it?" the Mem Sahib asked.

"Someone has died," answered the young officer. "You didn't tell me the cholera was already here among your servants!"

This was the first Mary had heard that cholera, a very deadly sickness, had broken out in the city. Her Ayah had been taken ill the night before and had just died. It was her death that set the servants wailing in fear. Mrs. Lennox and the young officer ran into the house, leaving poor Mary alone.

Mary ran and hid in her room. She was forgotten by everyone. She cried for a while and then slept for hours and hours.

When she awoke, the house was very quiet. Mary wondered if everybody had gotten well and all the trouble was over. She wondered who would take care of her now that her Ayah was gone. Mary was hungry and felt like no one cared about her. Surely someone would come to look for her. But no one came.

"How quiet it is," she said to herself. "It sounds as if there is no one here but me."

Then she heard footsteps. She could hear men talking in low voices outside her door.

"How sad!" she heard one voice say. "That pretty woman! And the child!"

A few minutes later, the men opened the door to Mary's room. One was a military officer she had seen once before with her father. He and his men were surprised to see her.

"Here is the child, all alone!" the officer cried.

"I am Mary Lennox," the little girl said, a little stiffly. "I fell asleep when everyone had the cholera and I just awoke. Why don't the servants come?"

One of the young men looked at her very sadly. "Poor little kid!" he said. "There is nobody left to come."

That was how Mary found out that both her mother and father had died. Some of the servants had died also, and the others had run away. That was why the place was so quiet.

Mary stayed for a while after that with an English minister and his family. He had five children who were always fighting. Mary did not like them at all. They didn't like *her*, either. One day when Mary was playing at making a garden, Basil, the minister's son, teased her:

"Mistress Mary, quite contrary,
How does your garden grow?
With silver bells, and cockleshells,
And marigolds all in a row."

After that, Basil and the rest of the children called her "Mistress Mary Quite Contrary" all the time.

The minister told Mary that she was going to sail to England and go live with her uncle, Mr. Archibald Craven. Mary had never heard of this uncle before, but he was the only family she had left. Basil teased Mary about this, too.

"He lives in a great big house in the country. No one goes near him because he's so cross. He's a hunchback, too!"

She didn't believe Basil. She put her fingers in her ears so she couldn't hear him.

Mary soon made the long voyage to England. An officer's wife took care of Mary on the ship, but she was busy with her own children and didn't pay much attention to contrary little Mary. In London, they were met by Mr. Craven's housekeeper, Mrs. Medlock.

Mary wondered about her uncle and where he lived. What sort of place was it? What would he be like? She felt very lonely.

They took a train to Yorkshire. Mary did not like Mrs. Medlock, but since she didn't like *anyone*, this wasn't unusual. Mary sat in the train car and looked out the window at the rain.

Mrs. Medlock did not like Mary, either. She thought the little girl was plain-looking and quite spoiled. Mrs. Medlock was the kind of woman who wouldn't take any nonsense from children. But Mr. Craven had sent her to fetch the girl, and that's what she did.

"I suppose I should tell you about where you are going," Mrs. Medlock said. "You are going to a gloomy place. The house is called Misselthwaite Manor. It's over six hundred years old. There are more than one hundred rooms in the house, but many are shut up and locked. The house is on the edge of the moor, with a big park and gardens around it. Mr. Craven's gloomy, too. I don't even know why he's bringing you there, because he is not going to trouble himself about you. He won't trouble himself about anyone. He's got a crooked back and that set him wrong. He's been even gloomier since his wife died. She was a pretty little thing."

Mrs. Medlock continued, "Most of the time Mr. Craven travels, far away from England. When he is at home, he stays shut up in his room. The only person he sees is his servant, Mr. Pitcher."

This did not make Mary feel cheerful—a house with its rooms shut up, and a man with a crooked back who shut himself up. She stared out of the train window at the pouring rain.

"You'll have to look after yourself," Mrs. Medlock warned. "You'll be told what rooms you can go into and what rooms you're to keep out of. Don't go wandering and poking about. Mr. Craven won't have it."

"I won't go poking about," said sour little Mary. She turned to face the window of the railway car and soon fell asleep.

CHAPTER TWO

Misselthwaite Manor

It was very dark when Mary woke up. The train had stopped at a station and Mrs. Medlock was shaking her.

"You have had a long sleep!" she said. "It's time to open your eyes! We're at Thwaite Station and we've got a long drive ahead of us."

They were the only ones who got off the train. A stylish carriage was waiting for them. The footman's long raincoat and hat were dripping with rain. He helped Mary into the carriage. She was curious about the house with the locked rooms, standing on the edge of a moor.

"What is a moor?" she asked Mrs. Medlock.

"Look out the window in a few minutes and you'll see," the woman answered. "You won't see much because it's a dark night, but you can see something."

Mary looked out the window. They drove through a tiny village. She saw cottages, shops, and a church. Then they were on the high road. She saw hedges and trees. There was nothing else to see for a long time. At last, the horses began to go more slowly, as if they were climbing uphill. There were no more hedges and no more trees. She could see nothing but darkness.

"We're on the moor now," said Mrs. Medlock.

Mary saw low bushes in the light from the carriage lamps. A wind made a wild, low, rushing sound. The darkness seemed to stretch out forever.

"It's not the sea, is it?" said Mary.

"No, it's not," answered Mrs. Medlock. "Nor is it fields or mountains. It's just miles and miles of wild land. Nothing grows here but heather and gorse. Nothing lives on it but wild ponies and sheep."

"It sounds like the sea," said Mary.

"That's the wind blowing through the bushes," Mrs. Medlock said. "It's a dreary place. But some people like it, especially when the heather blooms."

On and on they drove through the darkness.

I don't like it, Mary thought.

Finally Mary saw a light in the distance. The carriage drove on for a long time toward the light. At last they stopped in front of a long, low house. The big front door swung open. They entered a huge hall, with rows of pictures on the walls and suits of armor standing here and there. An elderly servant waited for them. He was Mr. Pitcher, the man who took care of Mary's uncle.

"Take her to her room," he told Mrs. Medlock. "Mr. Craven doesn't want to see her. He is going to London in the morning."

"Very well, Mr. Pitcher," she answered.

Mary followed Mrs. Medlock up the stairs and down a long hallway. They went up more stairs and through another hall and another. Finally, the housekeeper showed her into a bedroom.

"Well, here you are!" Mrs. Medlock said. "This room and the sitting room next to it are where you'll live. You must stay here. Don't forget!"

That was how Mary arrived at Misselthwaite Manor. She had never felt so contrary in all her life.

When she woke up the next morning, a young maid was lighting the fire in her room. Mary sat up in bed and looked around. It was a strange

room and kind of gloomy. The walls were covered with a tapestry that showed a forest scene. There was a castle in it, and hunters and horses and ladies. The windows had heavy, dark curtains on them. Outside, Mary saw a great stretch of land that looked like an endless purple sea.

"What is that?" she asked, pointing out the window.

Martha, the young maid, said, "That? That's the moor. It looks bare to thee now, but it's lovely when it's in flower. Then it smells like honey. Tha' will like it."

Mary thought that Martha sounded funny. Martha talked like most other people in Yorkshire, but the sound of it was strange to Mary's ears.

"Are you going to be my servant?" Mary asked. "Who is going to dress me?"

"Can't tha' dress thyself?" Martha asked, amazed.

"No," answered Mary. "I never did. My Ayah dressed me, of course."

"Well," said Martha, "it's time tha' learned. It'll do thee good to take care of thyself a bit."

Mary thought Martha wasn't a proper servant. She was right. Martha was a simple country girl,

working at the manor for money to help her family. There were twelve children in Martha's family and they lived in a tiny, four-room cottage. Everyone had to learn how to help out and do things for themselves. Martha didn't know what to do with a helpless girl like Mary, who didn't even know how to put her shoes on by herself!

As Mary struggled into her clothes, the friendly maid helped, chattering about her family.

"Tha' should see my brothers and sisters!" Martha said. "The younger ones tumble about, playing on the moor all day. Mother thinks it makes them healthy. My brother Dickon is twelve. He's a kind lad. Animals like him. He made friends with one of the wild moor ponies and now the pony follows him everywhere."

Mary had never had a pet of her own. She thought that she might like to have one. This made her think about Dickon, a boy who made friends with wild things. Since Mary had never thought about anyone but herself, this was a good beginning.

A large breakfast was waiting for Mary in the sitting room. She drank some tea and ate a little toast. Her appetite was always very small. Martha was shocked to see so much food wasted. In her family, there was usually not enough to fill them all up.

"Run out to play now," said Martha. "It'll do thee good."

"Out? Why?" Mary asked.

"Well, if tha' don't go out, what has tha' got to do?" Martha responded.

Mary looked around. There were no toys or books or games. Perhaps she would go see what the gardens were like.

"Who will go with me?" she asked.

Martha stared at her. "Tha' will go by thyself," she answered. "Our Dickon goes out and spends all day alone on the moor. He has a grand time, making friends with the animals. Tha' can go to the gardens." Martha waited for a few seconds, then added, "One of the gardens is locked up. It was Mrs. Craven's garden. When she died ten years ago, Mr. Craven locked the door and buried the key."

After that, Mary put on her coat and walked out into the main garden. She couldn't help thinking about the garden that had been locked up for ten years. Would everything in it be dead, or would there still be flowers?

She walked along the path, looking at the trees and evergreens. A large pool with an old fountain stood in the middle of the main garden. The fountain was not running. At the end of the path was a long wall, covered with ivy.

A door in the wall took her into a vegetable garden. The place was bare and ugly. It might be nice in summer, but there was nothing pretty about it now.

An old man with a spade over his shoulder walked toward Mary. He had a grumpy face.

"What is this place?" she asked him. "Can I come in here?"

"If tha' likes. But there's nothing to see."

Mary walked on down the path. She looked in other doors and saw more gardens. There were walls all around them. She followed the longest wall and found herself in an orchard with brown winter grass and bare fruit trees. She could see the tops of more trees above the wall, but there was no door to get into the garden where they were.

A bird with a bright red breast suddenly burst into song. His friendly whistle made Mary feel happy, which was quite a new feeling for her. She wondered: Does the bird know about the

locked-up garden? And why had Mr. Craven buried the key? If he had liked his wife so much, why did he hate her garden?

"I believe that bird flew into the secret garden," Mary said. "There was a wall around it but no door."

She walked back to the first garden and found the old man.

"I went into the other gardens and the orchard," she said.

"There was no dog at the door to bite thee," he answered.

"There was no door from the orchard into the other garden," said Mary.

"What garden?" he said in a rough voice.

"The one on the other side of the wall," answered Mistress Mary. "A bird with a red breast was sitting on one of the trees."

The old man smiled and whistled softly. The bird with the red breast flew to him.

"*Here* he is," chuckled the old man. He talked to the bird like it was an old friend. "Where has tha' been, little beggar?"

The bird looked at him without fear. He hopped about and pecked the earth, looking for seeds and insects.

"What kind of bird is he?" Mary asked.

"He's a robin redbreast. They're the friendliest birds alive. They hate to be lonely."

"I'm lonely," Mary told him. Seeing the robin made her think how much she'd like to have a friend.

The old gardener stared at her. "Art tha' the little girl from India?" he asked. Mary nodded. "No wonder tha' art lonely," he said.

"What is your name?" she asked.

"Ben Weatherstaff," he answered. "I'm lonely, too, except when the robin's with me. He's the only friend I've got."

"I have no friends at all," said Mary.

"Tha' and me are alike, then," he said. "We're neither of us good-looking and we're both sour as we look."

This was the first time anyone had spoken so plainly to Mary. She started to wonder why she was so sour.

Just then the robin flew away.

"He flew over the wall!" Mary cried out. "There must be a way to get into that secret garden!"

"Don't be nosy," the old man muttered. "Go on and play."

He walked off without even saying good-bye.

CHAPTER THREE

The Cry in the Corridor

Every morning after that, Mary went out to the gardens. There was nothing else to do. Playing out of doors was good for her. The fresh air put pink in her cheeks and made her hungry. She didn't look so sour anymore.

Everything in the gardens was still gray and wintry. She wondered what things would look like in springtime. Some days she looked for Ben Weatherstaff. Sometimes he would talk to her. Other times he would pick up his spade and walk away like he didn't see her.

Her favorite place was the long walk outside the gardens with the walls around them. Ivy hung down one of the walls in heavy curtains. One day she looked at the ivy and saw a flash of red and heard a chirp. There, on the top of the wall, was the robin.

"Oh!" she cried out. "Is it you?"

He chirped and hopped along the wall. It seemed to Mary that she understood him.

"Good morning!" he seemed to say. "Isn't the wind nice? Isn't the sun nice? Let's chirp and hop! Come on! Come on!"

Mary laughed. As he hopped, she ran after him.

"I like you!" she cried out. She chirped and tried to whistle. The robin chirped and whistled back at her.

He flew over the wall and perched in a tree.

"He's in the garden no one can go into," Mary said to herself. "He must live in there. I wish I could see what it is like!"

She walked back and forth along the wall. She looked hard, but there was no sign of a door.

"It's very strange," she said. "There must be a door, because Mr. Craven buried the key."

At supper that night, she asked Martha, "Why did Mr. Craven hate the garden?"

"I shouldn't talk about it," Martha said. "Mr. Craven's orders. He and his wife loved that garden. They planted roses and flowers all over it. One day his wife was sitting on a branch in an old tree in that garden. The branch broke. She fell and was hurt so bad that... well, she died not too long after. He nearly went crazy then. That's why he hates it."

Mary looked at the fire and listened to the wind whistle and moan around the old house. At that moment, a very good thing was happening to her. In fact, four good things had happened to her

since she came to the manor. First, she had talked with a robin and they understood each other. Second, she had played outdoors until her blood had grown warm. Third, the exercise she was getting made her hungry. Fourth, now that she had heard Mr. Craven's story, she knew what it was like to feel sorry for someone.

As she listened to the wind, she thought she heard something else. It was almost like a child crying somewhere. It was far away, but it was inside the house. She looked at Martha.

"Do you hear anyone crying?" Mary asked.

Martha looked surprised. "No," she said. "Sometimes the wind sounds like someone crying."

"But listen," said Mary. "That sound is in the house. It sounds like someone is crying."

Just then a draft blew the door of Mary's room open with a crash. The crying sound was plainer than ever.

"There!" said Mary. "It *is* someone crying, and it's a child!"

Martha ran and shut the door and turned the key. Then everything was quiet.

"It was the wind," said Martha. "Or it was the little kitchen maid. She's had a toothache all day."

Mary did not believe Martha was telling the truth.

The next day, Mary could not go outside because rain was pouring down.

"What do you do in your cottage when it rains like this?" she asked Martha.

"Try to keep from getting under each other's feet mostly," Martha answered. "Dickon always goes out to the moor. He doesn't mind the rain. He says he sees things on rainy days that don't show up when it's fair weather. He once found a little fox cub half-drowned and brought it home. He found a young crow another time and he brought it home, too. He fed them and took care of them. Now they're like pets."

"I've never had a pet. If I had a crow or a fox cub, I could play with it," said Mary. "But I have nothing here to play with."

"There are thousands of books in the library downstairs," said Martha. "Maybe Mrs. Medlock would let thee read some of them."

So Mary went looking for the library. She didn't wait to ask Mrs. Medlock. She didn't really care about the books, either. She wanted to explore the house with so many closed rooms. She wandered alone through narrow halls and

wide ones, upstairs and downstairs. It all felt empty, as if she was the only one there.

In one room she found a cabinet with little elephants made of ivory. Mary had seen carved ivory in India and she knew all about elephants. She played with these for a long time. Then she set the elephants in order and closed the cabinet.

She wandered until she felt tired. When she tried to find her way back to her own room, she got lost.

"I don't know which way to go. How still everything is!"

As Mary stood in the strange corridor, she heard a sound. It was a soft, childlike whine. Her heart beat faster. "It *is* crying," she said.

Suddenly, Mrs. Medlock came around the corner. When she saw Mary, she looked angry.

"What are you doing here?" Mrs. Medlock demanded. "What did I tell you?"

"I turned the wrong corner," explained Mary. "I heard someone crying."

"You did not," said the housekeeper. "Come back to your own room or I'll box your ears."

She took Mary's arm and pulled her up one passage and down another. Finally she pushed her into her own room.

"Now," she said, "you stay where you're told to stay or you'll find yourself locked up."

Mrs. Medlock went out and slammed the door. Mary was pale with rage.

"There *was* someone crying! There *was*!" she said to herself.

CHAPTER FOUR

The Key to the Garden

"Look at the moor! Look at the moor!" Mary called to Martha the next morning.

The rain had ended. A deep blue sky arched high over the moor. Mary had never dreamed of a sky so blue. In India, skies were hot and blazing. The moor itself looked softly blue instead of gloomy purple-black.

"Aye," Martha grinned. "The storm's over. Spring is on its way. Just wait and see. It will be blooming all over, buzzing with butterflies and bees. Tha' will want to stay out all day like Dickon does."

"I like Dickon," said Mary, "and I've never seen him."

"Well," said Martha, "the very birds like him, and the rabbits and wild sheep and ponies, too. I wonder what Dickon would think of thee?"

"He wouldn't like me," said Mary in her stiff little way. "No one does."

"How does tha' like thyself?" Martha asked her.

Mary thought for a moment. "Not at all," she answered.

"Mother said that to me once," Martha said. "I was in a bad temper. She said, 'Tha' stands there saying tha' don't like this one and tha' don't like that one. How does tha' like thyself?' It brought me to my senses in a minute."

Mary thought she would like Martha's mother. She sounded like a very wise person, and nice, too.

Martha left for her day off. She was going home to the cottage on the moor. She would help her mother with the washing and the baking, and then play with her little brothers and sisters.

Mary went out into the gardens. The sunshine made the whole place look different. She went into the first garden and found Ben Weatherstaff working there.

"Springtime's coming," he said. "Can tha' smell it?"

"I smell something nice and fresh and damp," she said.

"That's the good rich earth," he answered. "It's making ready to grow things. In the flower gardens, tha' will see bits of green spikes sticking out of the earth."

"What are they?" asked Mary.

"Crocuses and snowdrops and irises and daffydowndillys," Weatherstaff said. "Has tha' never seen them?"

"No, they don't have those flowers in India," said Mary.

She heard the soft rustling of wings. The robin had come again. He hopped about and looked at her. "Do you think he remembers me?" she asked.

"Of course!" said Weatherstaff. "He knows everything that goes on in the gardens!"

"Are things growing in that garden where he lives?" Mary inquired.

"What garden?" grunted Weatherstaff.

"The one that's locked up," she continued. "Are all the flowers dead? Are there ever any roses?"

"Ask him," said Weatherstaff, nodding toward the robin. "He's the only one that knows. No one else has seen inside it for ten years."

Mary walked through the gardens to the long, ivy-covered wall. She heard a chirp and a twitter. She looked down at the bare flowerbed. The robin had followed her. He was pecking things out of the earth.

"You *do* remember me!" she cried out.

She chirped and talked. He hopped and twittered. She bent down close to him and tried to make something like robin sounds. She was so happy that he let her get close to him!

The robin stopped to peck at a worm. As Mary watched, she saw something almost buried in the soil. It looked like a rusty old iron ring. She put out her hand and picked it up. It was an old key and it must have been buried a long time.

"Perhaps it has been buried for ten years," she said in a whisper. "Perhaps it is the key to the garden!"

She put the key in her pocket and looked at the wall. Could she find the door? All she could see was thick ivy. Mary took the key with her so she would be ready if she ever found the hidden door.

Martha was back the next morning, full of stories about her day off. She had helped her Mother with the baking and the washing. In the evening, Martha had told her family about the little girl from India.

"They wanted to know all about thee," said Martha. "I couldn't tell 'em enough!"

"I'll tell you more before your next day out," Mary promised. "They might like to hear about riding on elephants and camels, and hunting tigers. Did Dickon and your mother like to hear you talk about me?"

"Why, yes," answered Martha. "Mother was worried about thee. She said it must be hard to be all alone, with no nurse or governess to look after thee. She said, 'Martha, do thy best to cheer her up.' Here, I've brought thee a present!"

"A present!" exclaimed Mary. How could a cottage full of fourteen hungry people give anyone a present?

It was a skipping-rope with striped red and blue handles. "Mother bought it from a peddler," Martha explained. "She doesn't have any money to spare, but she wanted thee to have something to play with. She used some money from my wages."

"What is it for?" Mary asked.

"For!" cried out Martha. "Does tha' mean that they don't have skipping-ropes in India? Just watch me."

Martha began to skip, and skip, and skip. She counted to one hundred as she skipped.

"It looks nice," Mary said. "Your mother is very kind. Do you think I could skip like that?"

"Try it," urged Martha, handing Mary the skipping-rope. "Mother said it would do thee good. Put on a coat and go skip outside."

Mary took the skipping-rope. She opened the door, but turned back slowly.

"Martha," she said stiffly, "they were your wages. Thank you."

Martha laughed. "Run off outside and play."

The skipping-rope was a wonderful thing. Mary counted and skipped, and skipped and counted. The sun was shining. The wind came in delightful little gusts. She skipped all around the gardens. Ben Weatherstaff was talking to his robin. He was surprised to see Mary skipping.

"Well!" he exclaimed. "Tha' does look like a child now instead of a grumpy old lady. I wouldn't have believed thee could do it."

"I never skipped before," Mary said. "I can only go up to twenty."

"Tha' keep doing it. Just see how he's watching thee," Weatherstaff said, nodding toward the robin.

Mary skipped away. She went to the ivy wall to try to skip the whole length of it. When she stopped to rest, the robin greeted her with a chirp. He had followed her again. As she skipped toward him, Mary felt the key she kept in her pocket.

"You showed me where the key was yesterday," she said. "Will you show me the door today?"

The robin flew to the top of the wall. What happened next seemed like Magic.

A strong gust of wind lifted the trailing sprays of ivy, and Mary saw something. It was a door handle! She pulled the leaves aside. Her heart began to thump. It was the lock of the door that had been closed for ten years! She tried the key in the keyhole. It turned! She took a long breath, then slowly, slowly pushed open the door.

She slipped through and shut it behind her. She stood with her back against it, looking about her. She breathed quite fast with excitement, and wonder, and delight.

She was standing *inside* the secret garden!

CHAPTER FIVE

A Garden to Tend

It was the sweetest, most mysterious-looking place anyone could imagine. The high walls of the garden were covered with the branches of climbing roses. They were all gray, with no leaves or blossoms at all. They looked quite dead. The rose branches ran all over the trees in the garden, sometimes hanging down like curtains. They crept from one tree to another, making lovely bridges of themselves. It was different from any place Mary had ever seen in her life.

"How still it is!" she whispered.

She walked under one of the fairy-like arches between the trees.

"I wonder if they are all dead," she said.

She hoped they weren't. For here she was, inside the wonderful garden. She could come through the door under the ivy any time. She felt as if she had found a world all her own.

The robin flew down and hopped about, chirping, as if he were showing her things. Mary did not feel lonely at all, but she did hope the roses were not dead. How wonderful it would be with thousands of roses growing on every side!

She followed a grass path through the garden. In one corner she found an old flowerbed. Mary saw some little green points sticking up out of the earth. She thought perhaps these were flowers like Ben Weatherstaff had told her about.

"It isn't a dead garden," she said to herself. "Even if the roses are dead, there are other things alive—crocuses or snowdrops or daffodils."

The grass and weeds grew thick around the little green points. She found a sharp piece of wood and knelt down and dug out the weeds. Mary didn't know anything about gardening, but that was exactly the right thing to do.

"Now they can breathe," she said. "I am going to do more."

Mary worked in her garden until it was time for her midday dinner. She dug and dug. She found lots of little green points, and gave them all breathing room. Mary enjoyed herself very much.

"I will come back again," she said.

Then she slipped out the door and ran back into the house. Her cheeks were red and her eyes were bright when she sat down to dinner. She ate two pieces of meat and three helpings of rice pudding. Martha was delighted to see that the skipping-rope had been so good for her!

"I wish I had a little spade," Mary told Martha after dinner.

"What does tha' want a spade for?" asked Martha.

Mary did not want to tell Martha about the secret garden. What if Mr. Craven found out? He would be angry. He might get a new key and lock the garden up forever.

"This is such a big, lonely place," Mary said slowly. "If I had a little spade, I could make a little garden somewhere."

Martha's face lit up. "That's one of the things that Mother said. She wondered why no one had given thee a bit of a garden to take care of thyself! She thought it would make thee happy."

"How much would a spade cost?" Mary wanted to know.

"Well," Martha answered, "I saw little garden sets in the village for two shillings."

"I've got more than that," said Mary. Mrs. Medlock gave her a shilling a week for spending money, but so far she had had no reason to spend any of it.

"Our Dickon knows how to make things grow," Martha said. "We could write a note to him and ask him to buy garden tools and seeds. But tha' has to print plain because he can't read fancy writing."

Mary knew how to write fancy, but she could print if she had to. Martha told her what to say in the letter:

Dear Dickon:
Miss Mary has money. Will you go to Thwaite
village and buy her some flower seeds and a
set of garden tools? Give my love to Mother.

Your loving sister,
Martha Phoebe Sowerby

"We'll put the money in the envelope. Dickon will bring the things to thee himself."

"Oh," said Mary, "then I shall see him!"

After dinner, Mary was quiet and thoughtful. Just before Martha left, Mary asked her a question.

"Martha," Mary said, "has the kitchen maid had a toothache again today? When I was in the hall earlier, I heard that crying again. There's no wind today, so it couldn't have been the wind."

"There's Mrs. Medlock's bell. I must go," said Martha in a hurry, and she ran out.

"It's the strangest house anyone ever lived in," said Mary.

Fresh air and digging and skipping rope had made her so tired that she quickly fell asleep.

CHAPTER SIX

Dickon

Mary called it the Secret Garden. It seemed like a place out of a fairy tale. She tried to imagine it covered with blossoms. The sun shone all that week, and Mary was outside every day. All the digging and skipping rope was doing her good. She could run fast for a long time now and skip rope up to a hundred.

Sometimes she talked with Ben Weatherstaff. He seemed to like her better now. Maybe it was because Mary was starting to be a nicer little girl.

"If you wanted to make a garden," she asked him, "what would you plant?"

"Mostly roses," he answered. "And a few

vegetables. I don't need much."

"So you like roses?" she said.

"Aye, that I do. A young lady that I was gardener to had a lot of roses, and she loved them. That was ten years ago."

"Where is she now?" asked Mary.

"Heaven," he answered. "At least, that's what the parson says."

"What happened to the roses?" Mary asked.

"Why does tha' care so much about roses all of a sudden?" he demanded.

Mary's face grew red. She was afraid to answer. She did not want Ben Weatherstaff to know her secret.

"I want to play that I have a garden of my own," she said. "There is nothing for me to do and no one to play with. I want to pretend that I have a rose garden." Then she asked him as many questions as she dared. After a while, he got cross.

"Now look here! Don't ask so many questions," he said gruffly. He walked off.

Mary skipped to the woods near the secret garden to look for rabbits. There she saw a boy sitting under a tree, playing on a little wooden

flute. His hair was rusty brown and his cheeks were red as poppies. Mary had never seen such blue eyes. A brown squirrel was watching him. Two rabbits sat nearby, listening to him playing his flute.

"Don't move," he said quietly when he saw Mary. "It will scare them."

Mary stayed still. The boy stood up slowly and the rabbits hopped away.

"I'm Dickon," the boy said. "I know tha' art Miss Mary."

Mary had guessed that he was Dickon. Who else could it be, talking with the animals?

"I've got the garden tools and the seeds," he said. His smile spread all over his face. He took a little package out of his coat pocket. "There's a lot of poppies. They'll grow anywhere."

He turned his head. "Where's that robin that's calling us?"

"Is it really calling us?" she asked.

"Yes," said Dickon. "Whose is he?"

"He's Ben Weatherstaff's, but he knows me a little," answered Mary.

Dickon made a sound like the robin's own twitter. The robin listened and then answered.

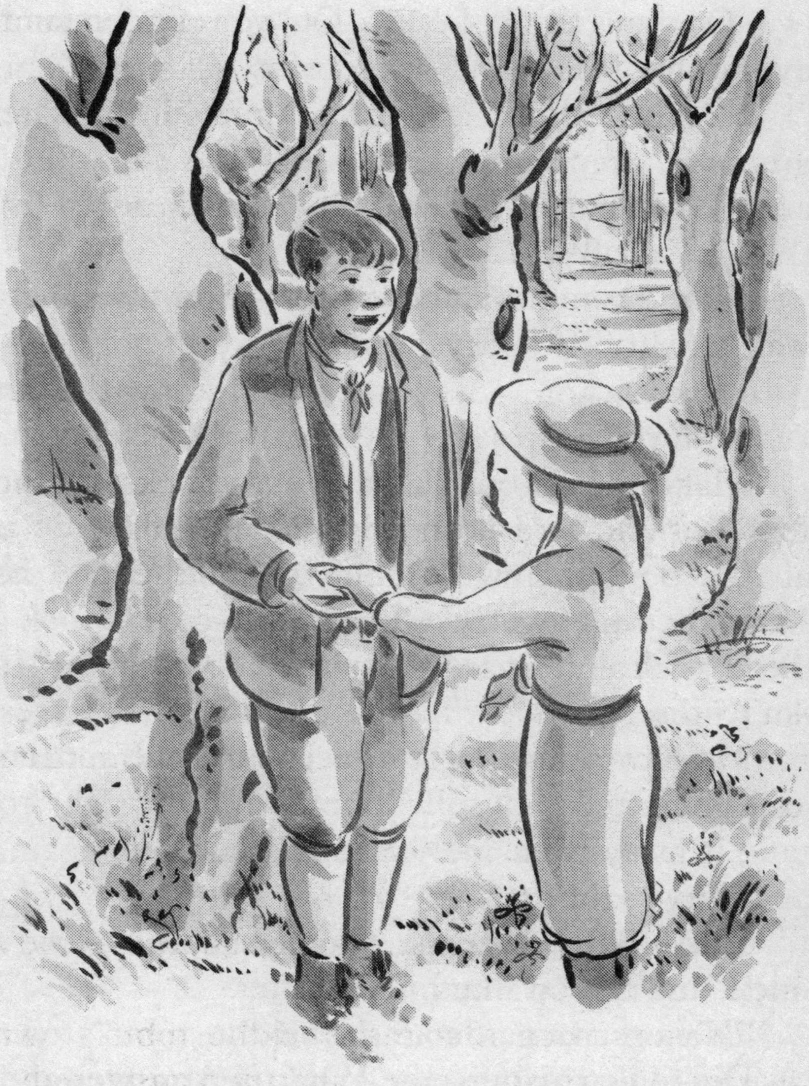

"He's thy friend, too," chuckled Dickon.

"Do you think he is? Do you understand everything birds say?" asked Mary.

"I think I do, and they think I do," he grinned. "Sometimes I think perhaps I'm a bird and I don't know it. Here, I'll plant the seeds for thee myself. Where is thy garden?"

Mary thought about it for a minute. She wasn't sure if she should share her secret with Dickon.

"Can you keep a secret?" she finally asked him.

Dickon answered, "I keep secrets about fox cubs and bird nests all the time. If I didn't, all the boys in town would bother them. Aye, I can keep secrets."

"I've stolen a garden," she said very fast. "It isn't mine. Nobody wants it and nobody cares for it. They're letting it die! I found the garden and got into it myself. They have no right to take it away from me!" She felt contrary again, and very stubborn.

Mary led him to the door, pushed it slowly open, and they walked in together.

"It's a secret garden," she said.

Dickon whispered, "What a strange and

beautiful place. It's like a dream. I never thought I'd see it."

"Did you know about it?" asked Mary.

"Aye, but no one was supposed to talk of it," Dickon answered.

"Are the roses still alive?" Mary asked. "Can you tell?"

"There's lots of dead wood that should be cut out, but they're alive," Dickon said. He bent down and cut a branch with his pocket knife. "When the wood is all gray and brittle, the rose is done for. When the wood looks greenish and juicy like this here, it's alive," he explained. "There'll be a fountain of roses here this summer."

They walked around the garden, talking softly so no one outside would hear. Mary showed Dickon the little green points growing up from the earth. She told him how she dug out the weeds.

"Why, a gardener couldn't have done better! These flowers will surely grow well now. Tha' has done a lot of work for such a little girl," Dickon said.

"I'm growing fatter and stronger, too," Mary answered. "When I dig, I'm not tired at all. I like to smell the earth when it's turned up."

Dickon agreed. "There's nothing like the smell of good earth and fresh growing things. I sniff until my nose quivers like a rabbit's, Mother says."

"Will you come again and help me work in the garden?" Mary begged.

"I'll come every day," he answered. "It's fun, waking up a garden. We'll talk to the robin, too."

He looked around thoughtfully. "Someone besides the robin has been in here since it was shut up ten years ago. Someone has pruned some of the roses."

"But the door was locked and the key was buried," said Mary. "No one could get in."

Dickon began to plant the seeds he had brought. Mary remembered what Basil had sung to tease her.

"Are there any flowers that look like bells?" she asked.

"Lilies of the valley do," he answered, "and there are Canterbury bells, and campanulas."

"Let's plant some," said Mary.

"There are lilies of the valley here already. Why does tha' want them?"

Then Mary told him about Basil calling her "Mistress Mary Quite Contrary," with a garden full of silver bells and cockleshells.

Dickon laughed.

"You are as nice as Martha said you were," Mary told him. "I like you, and that makes five people that I like. There's you, your mother, and Martha. Plus Ben Weatherstaff and the robin." Then she did something she had never done before. She asked Dickon, "Do you like me?"

"That I do!" he answered heartily. "I like thee, and so does the robin!"

The clock in the courtyard chimed noon.

"Run on and eat thy dinner," Dickon said. "I'll get some more work done before I start back home."

Mary went slowly toward the door. Then she turned back.

"You never would tell anyone about the garden, would you?" she asked.

"If tha' was a bird—a missel thrush—and showed me where thy nest was, does tha' think I'd tell anyone? Not me," said Dickon. "Tha' art as safe as a missel thrush." And she was sure she was.

Martha was waiting with Mary's dinner when she ran into her room.

"Where has tha' been?" Martha asked.

"I've seen Dickon!" said Mary happily.

"I knew he'd come," said Martha. "He's the best lad ever born. He brought thee the garden tools and the seeds, didn't he? Where will tha' plant thy flowers? Did tha' ask anyone?"

"I haven't asked anybody yet," said Mary slowly. Martha's question scared her. She was not ready to share her secret yet with anyone but Dickon.

After dinner, Martha said, "I've got something to tell thee. Mr. Craven came home this morning and I think he wants to see thee."

"What? Why?" Mary asked. Her face turned pale. "He didn't want to see me when I first came."

"Well," explained Martha, "Mother talked to him in the village yesterday. He wants to see thee before he goes away again."

Just then Mrs. Medlock opened the door and said, "Mary, come with me to Mr. Craven's study."

Mary's heart thumped. What would she say to Mr. Craven? She knew he would not like her, and she would not like him.

When they got to the study, Mr. Craven was sitting in an armchair in front of the fire.

"This is Miss Mary, sir," Mrs. Medlock said.

"Leave her here. I will ring when I want you to take her away," said Mr. Craven.

Mary stood waiting. The man in the chair was not a hunchback. His shoulders were high and rather crooked, but there was no hunch. He would have been handsome if he weren't so sad.

"Come here!" he said.

Mary went to him. He looked worried, as if he did not know what to do with her.

"Do they take good care of you here? I meant to get you a nurse or a governess, but I forgot," he said.

"Oh, please, no. I am too big for a nurse. Please don't make me have a governess yet."

"That's what Mrs. Sowerby said," he muttered.

"Is she Martha's mother?"

"Yes," he said. "She stopped me in the village yesterday. She said that you need to play and grow stronger before you start lessons. So what do you want to do?"

"I want to play outside," Mary answered.

"Perhaps it will do you good," he agreed. "Where do you play?"

"Everywhere," gasped Mary. She was afraid he might guess her secret. Then he would lock the garden again. "Martha's mother sent me a

skipping-rope. I skip and run. I don't do any harm," she said very quickly.

"Don't look so frightened," he said. "You could not do any harm. You may do what you like. I sent for you today because Mrs. Sowerby told me I should. I was surprised that she was bold enough to come up to me, but she said her daughter had talked about you. She also said that Mrs. Craven had been kind to her."

It was hard for him to say his dead wife's name.

"Is there anything you want?" he asked. "Do you want toys, books, dolls?"

"Might I," whispered Mary, "have a bit of earth?"

"Earth!" he repeated. "What do you mean?"

"To plant seeds in," Mary answered.

"A bit of earth," he said again. "You can have as much earth as you want. You remind me of someone else who loved things that grow. There! You must go now; I am tired. Good-bye. I will be gone all summer."

He rang the bell and Mrs. Medlock took Mary back to her room. Martha was waiting for her.

"I can have my garden!" Mary told her. "He is really a nice man, but his face is so sad."

Mary ran out to the garden. Dickon was not there.

"He's gone," she said. "Oh, was he only a wood fairy?"

Something on the rosebush caught her eye. It was a piece of paper, stuck onto a thorn. Dickon had left it there! There was a picture of a nest with a missel thrush sitting on it. There were roughly-printed words on it, too. It said, "I will com bak."

CHAPTER SEVEN

"I Am Colin"

Mary fell asleep that night looking forward to working in the garden the very next day. But she woke to hear the rain beating against her window. She hated the sound of it and was too miserable to go back to sleep.

Suddenly she heard another noise. "That isn't the wind," she whispered. "It's that crying I heard before." She must find out what it was! She got out of bed and put on her robe. She took a candle and crept out into the dark hallway.

Her heart beat fast as she walked through the halls. The faraway sound called to her. She went down one hallway and then another. She turned to the left. There was a door, and behind it someone *was* crying! It sounded like a very young someone. She pushed the door open to a large, dark bedroom. A candle burned by the bed.

There was a boy in the bed, crying. Mary crept toward him. He was very pale and thin, with huge gray eyes and long dark lashes. He looked at Mary with fear in his eyes.

"Who are you? Are you a ghost?" he whispered.

"No," Mary answered. "Are you?"

"No, I am Colin," he said, still frightened. "Who are you?"

"I am Mary Lennox. Mr. Craven is my uncle."

"He is my father," said the boy.

"Your father!" gasped Mary. "No one told me he had a boy!"

"Come here," he said. "Where did you come from?"

"I came to find out who was crying," Mary answered. "Why were you crying? Why did no one tell me you were here?"

"I was crying because my head ached," Colin answered. "I am always sick. If I live, I may be a hunchback, but I won't live. I won't let people look at me and laugh."

"Does your father come and see you?" Mary asked.

"He doesn't want to see me."

"Why?"

"My mother died just after I was born and it makes him miserable to look at me," Colin said angrily.

"If you don't like people to see you, do you want me to go away?" Mary asked.

"No," he said. "I want to hear about you. Why you came here, if you like it, and where you lived before."

She answered all his questions. She could see that he was very spoiled. He had lots of books and toys, but nothing seemed to amuse him.

"Everyone must do what pleases me," he said. "It makes me ill to be angry. Everyone thinks I will die before I grow up. How old are you?" he asked.

"I am ten," answered Mary, and then she thought for a moment. "And you must be ten, too. For, just after you were born, the garden door was locked and the key was buried. And it has been locked for ten years."

"What garden door was locked? What key?" he demanded.

"The garden Mr. Craven hates—but the door

is hidden now," Mary answered carefully. She did not want to mention Colin's dead mother. She also wasn't sure that she could trust Colin with her secret. She didn't want him to know that she had already found the garden.

Colin liked the idea of a hidden garden. He asked question after question.

Mary wanted to change the subject. "Do you think you *really* won't live?" she asked at last.

"I don't suppose I will," he answered calmly. "Everyone says I won't."

"Were you crying about that?" Mary asked.

"Yes, but let's talk about something else," he said. "Tell me about the garden. I want to see it. I will make the servants take me out to find it."

"Oh, no, we must keep it a secret!" she cried out. "If we can find the door, we'll be able to pretend it's our garden. We can plant seeds and make everything come alive again in the spring."

"Is the spring coming?" he said. "What is it like? I've never seen it, because I've always been ill."

"It is the sun shining and flowers pushing up through the earth," said Mary.

"I never had a secret," he said. "I like the idea of keeping the garden secret."

"Maybe," said Mary, "we can find some boy who would push your wheelchair to the garden. I'll tell you what I think it would be like, if we could go into it. It has been shut up so long that things have probably grown into a tangle."

He listened while she talked about the roses and birds they might find there. He even smiled. Then he gave her a surprise.

"Do you see that silk curtain on the wall over the fireplace?" he asked. "There is a cord hanging from it. Go pull it."

Mary pulled the cord. Behind the curtain was a picture of a very young lady with a laughing face. Her lovely gray eyes were exactly like Colin's unhappy ones.

"She is my mother," said Colin. "Sometimes I hate her for dying. If she had lived, I think I would be healthy. And my father wouldn't have hated to look at me. Close the curtain. I don't like to see her laughing when I am so miserable."

Colin asked Mary to visit him every day and she promised that she would. She felt sorry for him, so she stayed and sang softly to him while he fell asleep.

"I found out what the crying was," Mary told Martha the next morning. "It was Colin. I found him."

"Oh, Miss Mary!" Martha said, half crying. "Tha' shouldn't have done it! Tha'll get me in trouble. I shall lose my job!"

"You won't lose your job," said Mary. "He was glad I came. He asked me questions and let me see his mother's picture. I sang him to sleep."

"Dost tha' mean to say," cried Martha with wide open eyes, "that he was nice to thee?"

"I think he liked me," Mary answered. "What is the matter with him?"

"Nobody knows for sure," said Martha. "Mr. Craven wouldn't set eyes on him after Mrs. Craven died. He said the baby would be a hunchback like him."

"Is Colin a hunchback?" Mary asked. "He didn't look like one."

"He isn't yet," said Martha. "They think that his back is weak. They never let him walk. Once a great doctor came from London and said there'd been too much medicine and that he was too spoiled."

"Do you think he will die?" asked Mary.

"Mother says there's no reason why he should

live," Martha answered. "He does nothing but lie in bed and he does get sick easily. He gets no fresh air. He hates being taken outside."

"I wonder," Mary said slowly, "if it would help him to go out into a garden."

"One of the worst fits he ever had," said Martha, "was when they took him out to the garden."

Very soon afterward, Martha was called to Colin's room. She came back looking puzzled.

"Well," she said, "the minute the nurse left, Colin said to me, 'Go get Mary Lennox, and don't tell anyone.' "

Mary went quickly.

"Come in," Colin said. "I've been thinking about you all morning."

Mary told Colin about Dickon. "He is Martha's brother," she said. "He is twelve years old. He can charm foxes and squirrels and birds. He and the robin talk to each other in soft chirps. He knows all about eggs and nests. And he knows where foxes and badgers and otters live. Dickon knows about everything that lives on the moor. He's always looking up in the sky to watch birds flying, or looking down to see something

growing. He laughs such a big laugh and his cheeks are red as cherries."

It was the best thing Mary could have done. Talking about Dickon, the moor, and the garden took Colin's mind off dying. They had such fun talking that they began laughing. No one would have recognized unlovable little Mary and poor sick Colin then. They looked almost like normal children.

"Do you know what?" Colin asked. "We are cousins." With all their talking, that is the one thing they had not thought of. They laughed more than ever.

In the middle of their fun, the door opened. Mrs. Medlock walked in with the doctor, who was Mr. Craven's brother. Mrs. Medlock was frightened to see Mary there. Dr. Craven was very surprised.

"What is this?" demanded Dr. Craven.

Mary had once seen a boy in India who was a prince. He wore fine clothes and many jewels. Everybody had to do what *he* told them to do. Suddenly, Colin reminded Mary very much of that prince.

"This is my cousin, Mary Lennox," Colin

announced. "I like her. She must come and talk to me whenever I send for her. She makes me better. Last night, she sang me to sleep."

Mrs. Medlock and Dr. Craven were amazed to hear this, but they could see that Colin did look a little better. Still, Dr. Craven warned Colin. He must not forget that he was ill or that he got tired easily.

"I *want* to forget it," Colin fretted. "She makes me forget it. That's why I want her."

Dr. Craven left, completely puzzled.

Colin turned to Mary. "Tell me about India," he said.

CHAPTER EIGHT

Nest Building

It rained every day for a week. Mary spent hours each day with Colin, talking about gardens or Dickon or what it was like to live in India. Yet all the while they talked, she was wondering if Colin could be trusted with the secret about the garden.

If he could be trusted, would it be possible to take him to the garden without having anyone find it out? Perhaps if he had fresh air and knew Dickon and the robin and saw things growing, he might not think so much about dying. But if he hated for people to look at him, perhaps he would not like to see Dickon.

"Why does it make you angry when you are looked at?" she asked Colin one day. "Would you hate it if a boy looked at you?"

"There's one boy I believe I wouldn't mind. Dickon. He's a sort of animal charmer, and I am a boy animal."

They both laughed. Mary knew then that Dickon and Colin would get along fine.

The next morning, Mary jumped out of bed and ran to the window. She put her hand out in the sunshine.

"It's warm!" she said. She flew outside and looked up in the sky. It was blue and pink and pearly and white. She ran toward the secret garden.

"Today Dickon will surely come," she said.

When she reached the door to the secret garden, she was startled by a loud sound. It was the caw-caw of a crow. She looked up and there sat a big black bird. Then he spread his wings and flapped away. She pushed the door open.

In the garden, the crow perched on an apple tree. A little reddish animal with a bushy tail was lying under the tree. It was a fox. Dickon was working hard nearby. Mary ran across the grass to him.

"Oh, Dickon!" she cried out. "When did you get here?"

"I was up long before the sun," he said. "How could I have stayed in bed? The world's all humming and nest-building. Why, the garden was lying here waiting!"

The little fox came over to him. The crow flew down and settled quietly on his shoulder.

"This," he said, rubbing the fox's head, "is Captain. And this," nodding at the crow, "is Soot."

There was every joy on earth in the secret garden that morning. When the robin flew across the wall with something in his beak, Dickon stood very still.

"He's building his nest," Dickon whispered. "He'll stay here if we don't scare him. When he's gotten used to us, I'll chirp a bit and he'll know we won't be in his way. It's part of the springtime, this nest-building is. A body had better not meddle. Let's talk about something else so he won't think we're looking at him."

Mary whispered quietly, "Do you know about Colin?"

"How did tha' find out about him?" Dickon asked.

Mary told him about the midnight wind and the faraway crying. She told how they talked, and how she worried because Colin thought so much about dying. Dickon looked slowly around the garden. It was no longer gray, but turning green.

"If Colin was out here," Dickon said, "he wouldn't be thinking about dying. Could we ever get him to come out here?"

"You could push his wheelchair," Mary said in a rush. "He could order the gardeners to keep away so they wouldn't find out."

"It'd be good for him," he said. "Have you noticed how the robin and his mate have been working?" He whistled, and the robin turned his head, still holding his twig. "We're nest-building too, bless thee. Look out tha' dost not tell on us."

Mary knew that the robin would keep their secret.

"I Won't!" Said Mary

Mary stayed in the sunny garden all day. At sunset, she ran back to the house to tell Colin about Dickon's fox cub and the crow. When she opened the door of her room, Martha was waiting for her with a grim face.

"What is the matter?" Mary asked.

"Colin had one of his tantrums," Martha answered. "He was angry because tha' didn't come see him today."

Mary ate her supper and then she finally went to see Colin. He was lying flat on his back in bed. Mary marched up to him. "Why didn't you get up?" she demanded.

"I got up this morning when I thought you were coming," he answered. "Then you didn't come. They put me back in bed this afternoon. Why didn't you come?"

"I was working in the garden with Dickon."

"I won't let him come here if you go play with him instead of coming to talk to me," he said with a frown.

"If you send Dickon away, I'll never come into this room again! I'll never come to talk with you, ever!" she shouted.

"I'll make you," said Colin. "The servants must do what I say. They shall drag you in."

"They may drag me in, Prince Colin," said Mary fiercely, "but I won't talk to you when I get here. I'll never tell you one thing!"

"You are a selfish thing!" cried Colin.

"You're more selfish than I am," Mary shouted.

"I'm not!" snapped Colin. "I'm not as selfish as Dickon is! He keeps you playing when he knows I am all by myself."

"He's nicer than any other boy that ever lived!" she said. "He's like an angel!"

"A nice angel!" Colin sneered. "He's a common cottage boy off the moor!"

"He's better than you with your princely ways!" retorted Mary.

A big tear ran down Colin's cheek. He felt sorry for himself.

"I'm not selfish! It's just that I'm ill and I'm sure there is a lump coming on my back," he said. "Everyone knows I am going to die."

"I don't believe it!" said Mary sourly. "You just say that to make people feel sorry for you."

"Get out!" he shouted, and he threw his pillow at her.

"I'm going," she said. "And I won't come back! I won't!" Before she went out the door, she turned back and said, "I was going to tell you all about Dickon and his fox and his crow, but now I won't tell you a single thing!"

She slammed the door. The nurse was outside, laughing.

"What are you laughing at?" Mary asked her.

"At you two," said the nurse. "It's about time someone stood up to him. Hysterics and temper are half what ails him."

"What are hysterics?" asked Mary.

"You'll find out if you work him into one of his fits," the nurse said.

Mary did not feel at all sorry for Colin. He could stay in his room and never get any fresh air and die if he liked! It would serve him right!

Martha was waiting in Mary's room. There was a wooden box on the table that Mr. Craven had sent. Mary opened the package. There were flower and garden books and games inside, and a fancy pencil case. Everything was so nice! If she had been friends with Colin, she would have run to show him her presents. They would have read the books and played the games. He would never once have thought about dying.

"He always thinks about it when he's tired," she said to herself. "I said I would never go back again, but maybe I will go in the morning. He may throw his pillow at me again, but I'll go."

In the middle of the night, Mary was awakened by dreadful sounds. Doors slammed. Footsteps hurried up and down the hall, and someone was screaming.

"It's Colin! He's having one of those fits the nurse calls hysterics. How awful it sounds. I can't bear it!" Mary said, and she covered her ears with her pillow.

The screams got louder. "Somebody ought to make him stop!" Mary cried out.

Mary got out of bed and ran angrily down the hall. She slapped Colin's door open and ran in past the nurse. Mary ran right up to the bed.

"You stop!" she shouted. "You stop! I hate you! Everybody hates you! You will scream yourself to death in a minute, and I wish you would! If you scream another scream, I'll scream too, and I can scream louder than you can and I'll frighten you!"

Colin was lying on his face in bed, beating his hands against the pillows. Tears were streaming down his face and he shook all over. Mary's angry words shocked him.

THE SECRET GARDEN

"I can't stop!" he sobbed. "I felt the lump! I felt it! I have a hunch on my back and I shall die."

"You didn't feel a lump!" said Mary fiercely. "There's nothing the matter with your back, nothing but hysterics! Turn your back this way and let me look at it!"

The nurse helped Colin roll over. His back was so skinny and white! Mary could count every rib and backbone knob on it. She looked up and down his spine, as closely as if she had been a great doctor from London.

"There's not a single lump there!" she said at last. "There's not a lump as big as a pin. If you ever say there is again, I shall laugh!"

Great tears streamed down his face. Colin was relieved. He had worried so much about lumps on his back that he had been afraid to ask anyone to look. Even the nurse didn't know that he had been scared about this.

"Do you think I could live to grow up?" he asked the nurse.

"I think you will. But you have to control your temper and get out in the fresh air," she told him.

He put out his hand toward Mary. "I'll go outside with you, Mary. I won't hate fresh air if

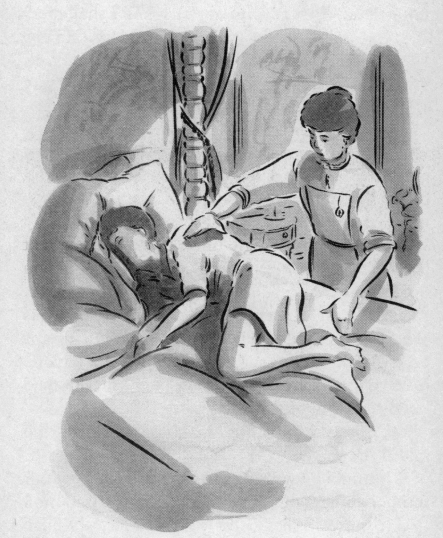

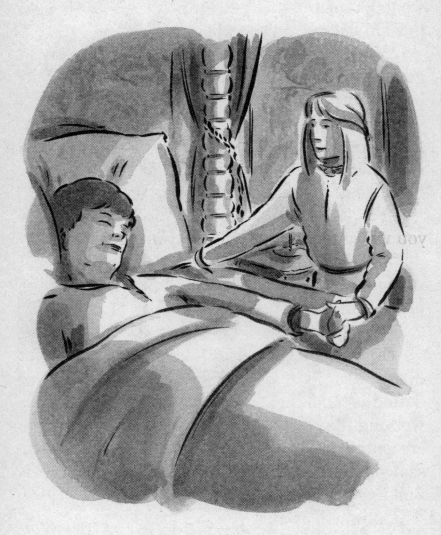

we can find—" then he whispered so the nurse wouldn't hear, "—the secret garden. I do so want to see Dickon and the fox and the crow."

"Would you like me to sing to you, so you can go back to sleep?" Mary whispered. She held his hand gently.

"Oh, yes!" he answered. The nurse left the room, smiling. Colin looked up at Mary. "You said you had a whole lot of nice things to tell me. Have you found the way into the secret garden?"

"Yes," she answered, "I think I have. And if you will go to sleep I will tell you tomorrow."

"Oh, Mary!" he said. "If I could get into it, I think I would live to grow up! Instead of singing, just tell me what you think it looks like inside."

She began to speak very slowly in a quiet voice.

"I think that roses have climbed over everything, like a mist. The ground is full of daffodils and snowdrops and lilies and irises working their way out of the dark. Perhaps there are purple and gold crocuses. And perhaps," she said very softly, "the robin has found a mate and is building a nest."

Colin was asleep.

CHAPTER TEN

"We Mustn't Waste Any Time"

Mary stopped to see Colin on her way to the garden the next morning. He was tired and achy from his tantrum, but in a good mood. He told her that he had dreamed about the garden all night, about tiny green leaves and birds on their nests.

Dickon was waiting for Mary in the garden. He had ridden his pony, Jump, over the moor. The pony nuzzled Mary's cheek. Dickon also had the fox and the crow with him. In his pockets, he had two tame squirrels named Nut and Shell. They scampered up and sat on Dickon's shoulders.

Mary told Dickon about Colin's tantrum. She could tell he felt very sorry for Colin.

"Springtime is coming. Just listen to those birds!" he said. "And that poor lad lying shut up! We must get him out here, sniffing the air. That would keep him from thinking about dying, I'll bet. We must get him just soaked through with sunshine. And we mustn't waste any time doing it."

"I'll tell you what we can do," Mary said. "He wants to meet you and see Soot and Captain. Tomorrow you could bring the creatures to him and we can make plans for bringing him out to the garden!"

It was hard to go back in the house that afternoon. When Mary went inside, she went straight to Colin's room. Colin sniffed when she came closer to him.

"What is that smell?" he cried out joyously. "It's cool and warm and sweet, all at the same time."

"It's the wind from the moor," said Mary. "It's the springtime and sunshine that smell so grand."

Colin began to laugh. She began to laugh, too. They laughed until they could not stop. Out in the hall, Mrs. Medlock was amazed to hear them.

Colin listened as Mary told all about Dickon and Captain and Soot and Nut and Shell and Jump. She told him how Jump had given her a

kiss on her cheek with his velvet nose.

"I wish I had friends like Dickon does," he said, "but I never had any friends."

"Dickon would be your friend," Mary said.

"I'd like that," said Colin. "I won't mind Dickon looking at me."

"I'm glad you said that. Can I trust you, for sure?" she begged.

"Yes, yes!" he whispered.

"Dickon will come to see you tomorrow morning, and he'll bring his creatures with him. But that's not all," Mary went on. "There is a door into the garden. I found it!"

"Oh, Mary!" he cried out. "Will I see it? Will I live to get into it?"

"Of course you'll see it!" snapped Mary. "Don't be silly!"

She began telling him what the secret garden was really, truly like. Colin forgot how tired he was as he listened.

"It is just what you thought it would be," he said at last. "It sounds just like you described it before. How did you know then what it was like?"

Mary boldly spoke the truth. "I had seen it, and I had been in it," she said. "I found the key

and got in weeks ago. But I didn't dare tell you until I could trust you for sure!"

Later that day, Dr. Craven came to see his poor, ill nephew Colin. He always came after there was a tantrum. Dr. Craven was surprised this time at what he found. Colin was sitting up straight on the sofa, talking with Mary. They were looking at pictures in a garden book. Their faces were happy and glowing.

"I heard you were ill last night, my boy," said Dr. Craven.

"I'm much better now," Colin answered. "I'm going outside soon. I want some fresh air."

Since Colin had always been terrified of going outside, this was another surprise for Dr. Craven. He felt Colin's pulse. "It must be a very nice day," the doctor said, "and you must not get tired."

"Fresh air won't tire me," said Prince Colin.

"I thought you did not like fresh air."

"I don't when I am alone," replied the Prince, "but my cousin is going out with me. She knows how to take care of me. A boy I know will push my wheelchair."

"It must be a strong and steady boy," Dr. Craven said.

"It's Dickon," Mary said at once.

Dr. Craven smiled. "Oh, if it is Dickon, you will be safe enough. Did you take your sleeping medicine last night?"

"No," Colin answered. "Mary talked me to sleep, telling me about Spring in a garden."

"That sounds nice," said Dr. Craven. "You must remember…"

"I don't want to remember. I want to forget," snapped the Prince. "My cousin makes me forget my aches and pains. That makes me better."

The doctor didn't know what to say. Colin was changing and he seemed to be getting better. It was Dr. Craven's shortest visit ever. He did not leave any new orders or medicine.

The next morning, Colin woke up thinking about the garden and Dickon and his wild creatures. Soon Mary burst into the room.

"It's so beautiful!" she said. "You never saw anything so beautiful! It has come, the Spring! Dickon says so!"

"Open the window," cried Colin.

Mary opened the window, letting freshness and scents and bird songs pour through.

"That's fresh air," she said. "Dickon says it makes him feel as if he could live forever and ever. Breathe it! There are buds on everything. The birds are in a hurry about their nests. Dickon brought his creatures—even a newborn lamb!"

When the nurse came in, Colin told her, "A boy, a fox, a crow, two squirrels, and a newborn lamb are coming to see me. Tell Martha to bring them here. The boy is Martha's brother, Dickon. He is an animal charmer."

"When do you think Dickon will come?" Colin asked Mary after breakfast.

They didn't have to wait long.

"Listen!" Mary said. "Did you hear a caw? That's Soot. Listen again. Do you hear a tiny bleat?"

"Oh, yes!" cried Colin.

"That's the lamb," said Mary. "He's coming."

Martha opened the door. "If you please, sir, here's Dickon and his creatures."

Dickon came in smiling. The lamb was in his arms. Captain, the little red fox, trotted by his side. Nut and Soot sat on his shoulders. Shell's head peeped out of his coat pocket. Colin stared in delight.

While they talked, Soot flew in and out of the open window. Nut and Shell scampered over the tree trunks and branches outside the window. Captain curled up near Dickon. The lamb rested on Colin's lap and Dickon showed the boy how to give him a bottle. Then the children made a plan to take Colin outside.

"I'm going to see the garden," cried Colin. "I am going to see it!"

CHAPTER ELEVEN

"I Shall Live Forever and Ever and Ever!"

But they had to wait more than a week to get out there. First it was windy outside, then Colin caught a cold. But every day, Dickon came to talk about the moor. He told about the houses of otters and badgers and about bird nests, and field mice and their burrows. The children made secret plans. Nothing must spoil the mystery of the garden. They planned to go to the garden in a roundabout way, so no one would know. There was only one problem. They had to fool the gardeners, too. Colin decided that he would just order them to stay away.

He called the head gardener to his room. When he got there, the gardener was surprised to see that Colin was sitting in an armchair. Dickon was feeding the lamb. A squirrel perched on Dickon's back, eating a nut. The little girl from India was sitting on a big footstool.

"I want to give you some very important orders," Colin told him in his princely way. "I am going out in my chair this afternoon. You know I hate to be stared at. None of the gardeners is to be anywhere near the garden walls. I will go out about two o'clock. Everyone must keep away."

"Very good, sir. Thank you, sir," said the head gardener. Then he left.

"It's all safe now," Colin said. "And this afternoon I shall see it!"

Dickon went back to the garden and Mary stayed with Colin. A little later, the nurse got Colin ready. He talked and laughed with Mary the whole time. The footman carried Colin downstairs and put him in his wheelchair. Dickon pushed the chair slowly and steadily. Mary walked beside it. Colin leaned back and lifted his face to the sky. The wind swept in soft, big breaths from the moor.

No one was in sight. When the children came to the garden walls, they spoke in whispers.

"This is it," breathed Mary. "This is where I used to walk up and down and wonder and wonder."

"Is it?" cried Colin. His eyes searched the wall eagerly. "But there is no door."

A few yards more and Mary whispered, "This is where the robin flew over the wall."

"Oh, I wish he'd come again!" cried Colin.

Dickon stood still and the wheelchair stopped.

"And this," said Mary, "is where he chirped at me from the top of the wall. And this is the ivy the wind blew back." She took hold of the green curtain and pulled it aside.

Colin gasped.

"And here is the handle, and here is the door. Dickon, push him in quickly!" Mary whispered.

Dickon pushed. Colin covered his eyes until they were inside, then he looked around and around. Tender little leaves had crept over everything. The flowers were splashes of gold and purple and white. The trees above his head were covered with pink buds. Everywhere wings fluttered and insects hummed. The sun was warm upon his face.

"I shall get well here!" he cried out. "Mary! Dickon! I shall get well! And I shall live forever and ever and *ever*!"

The children played in the garden all afternoon. Colin looked at all the wonders springing out of the earth or trailing down from trees. They looked for the robin.

"Tha' will see him after a bit," said Dickon. "He and his mate are very busy right now. When the eggs hatch, tha'll see him carrying worms as big as he is."

This made them giggle. They covered their mouths with their hands so no one would hear them.

Mary and Dickon were scared when Colin asked about the old tree. He saw that a large branch was missing. It was the branch that his mother had sat on. It was the branch that had fallen... But Colin didn't know about that. Instead, Dickon told Colin that roses would soon cover all the old dead wood of the tree. It would be the most beautiful spot in the whole garden. Just then, the robin flew past with a worm in his beak. Colin laughed, and he didn't ask about the tree any more.

"The robin's taking tea to his mate," Colin said. "I think I'd like some tea myself."

"It was Magic that sent the robin," Mary whispered to Dickon afterward. "It kept him from asking any more about the tree."

Colin asked Mary and Dickon to go to the house and bring back afternoon tea. They brought hot tea and cakes, and they all ate. Even Nut and Shell had pieces of cake. Soot took half of a crumpet and swallowed it in one gulp.

"I don't want this afternoon to end," Colin said, "but I shall come back tomorrow and every day after. I've seen the Spring and I'm going to see the Summer. I'm going to see everything grow. I'm going to grow here myself and get well."

"That tha' will," said Dickon. "Tha' will be walking around and digging before long." Dickon paused. "Tha' does have legs o' thine own, same as other folks…"

"There's nothing wrong with my legs," stated Colin. "They're just weak. I'm afraid to try to stand or walk."

"When tha' stops being afraid, tha'll stand on 'em," Dickon said with cheer.

The sun was dropping lower. The day was growing quiet. Colin suddenly whispered, "Who is that man?"

Colin pointed to the high wall. It was Ben Weatherstaff, staring over the wall from a ladder! He shook his fist at Mary.

"Tha'!" he cried, "Always poking thy nose where it isn't wanted!"

"Ben Weatherstaff, it was the robin who showed me the way!" called out Mary.

"Wheel me over there!" Colin told Dickon. "Stop right in front of him!"

Ben Weatherstaff saw the wheelchair coming toward him and his jaw dropped.

Colin held out his hand like a prince. "Do you know who I am?" he demanded.

Ben Weatherstaff stared as if he were seeing a ghost. He answered in a squeaky voice, "Aye, that I do. Tha' art the poor cripple."

"I'm not a cripple!" Colin cried out furiously.

"Tha' hasn't got a crooked back?" Ben said hoarsely. "Tha' hasn't got crooked legs?"

"No!" shouted Colin. "Come here!" he called to Dickon. Colin threw the blankets off his legs. Dickon was by his side in a second.

"He can do it! He can do it! He can do it! He can!" Mary whispered to herself. She wanted to make Magic, to keep him on his feet.

Suddenly Colin stood up out of his wheelchair. His feet and legs were very thin, but he stood straight as an arrow. His eyes flashed lightning.

"Look at me!" he cried to Ben Weatherstaff. "Just look at me!"

Tears ran down old Ben Weatherstaff's wrinkled cheeks.

"I'm your master," Colin said, standing even straighter, "when my father is away. This is my garden. Don't dare say a word about it! Come in here. I want to talk to you."

Ben whispered, "Yes, sir!"

Colin turned to Mary. "Go and meet him," he said. "Bring him in here to me."

Mary ran to the door under the ivy. Dickon watched Colin with sharp eyes. He showed no signs of falling. He was standing straight and strong.

"I can stand," he said, quite grandly.

"I knew tha' could as soon as tha' stopped being afraid," answered Dickon.

"Yes, I've stopped," said Colin. "Are you making Magic?"

Dickon's mouth spread in a cheerful grin. "Tha's doing Magic thyself. It's the same Magic that makes the flowers come up out of the earth."

"I'm going to walk to that tree," Colin said, and he did it. He looked tall. Ben Weatherstaff came in and looked at him in amazement.

Mary muttered, under her breath, "I knew you could do it!"

Colin stared at Ben Weatherstaff. "Look at me! Am I a hunchback? Have I got crooked legs?"

"No, sir!" the gardener answered. "Nothing of the sort. Why has tha' been hiding, letting people think tha' was crippled?"

"Everyone thought I was going to die," said Colin shortly. "I'm not!"

Ben Weatherstaff looked him over, up and down, down and up. "Nothing of the sort! Tha' art too plucky!"

"What work do you do in the gardens, Weatherstaff?" Colin asked.

"Anything I'm told to do," the old man answered. "I'm kept on because Mrs. Craven liked me."

"My mother?" said Colin. "This was *her* garden, wasn't it?"

"Aye," Ben answered, "she was very fond of it. She planted all the roses, she and Mr. Craven."

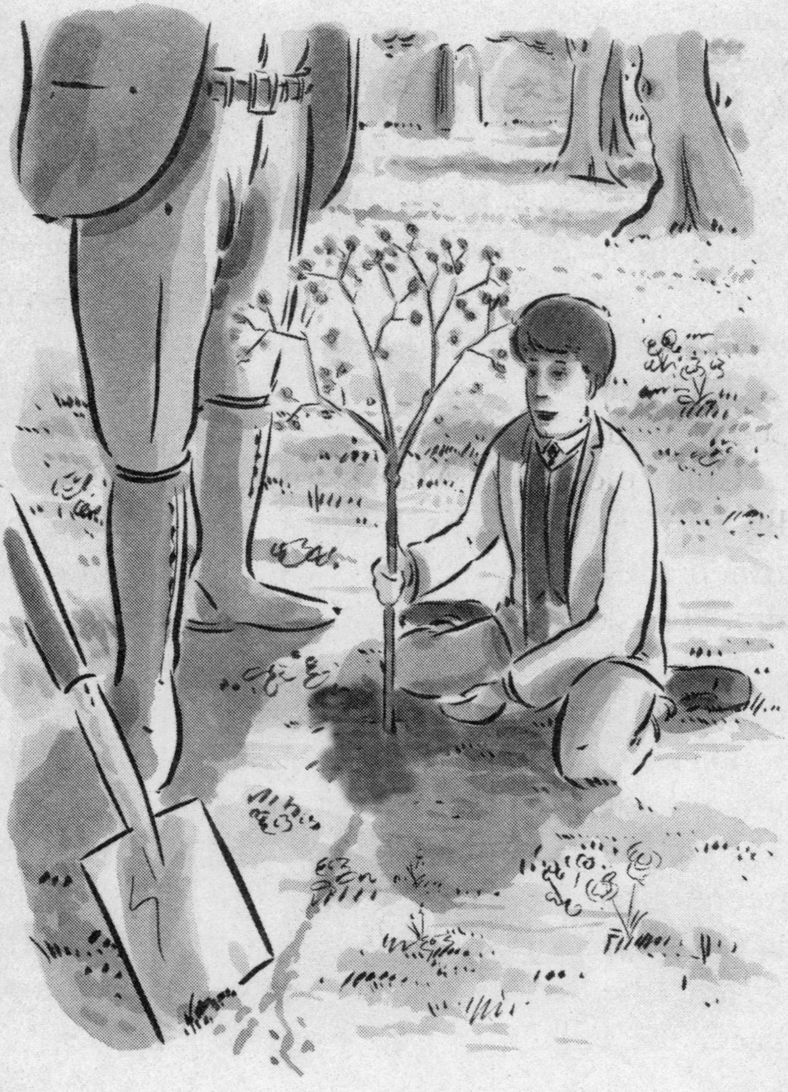

"It is my garden now. I am fond of it," said Colin. "My orders are for you to keep it a secret. Sometimes you can help with the gardening, but no one must know that you come."

"I've come here before when no one saw me," Weatherstaff said. "The last time I was here was about two years ago. I climbed over the wall. I came in to prune the roses. The last two years or so, I've been too stiff to climb over."

"I'm glad you did it, Weatherstaff," said Colin. "You'll know how to keep the secret."

Colin picked up Mary's trowel. He began to dig in the earth. His hand was weak, but he turned the soil over. Ben Weatherstaff watched him. He asked Colin if he'd like to plant a rose.

"Oh, yes, go and get it!" said Colin. "Quick!" Colin wanted to plant the rose before the sun set.

Dickon helped Colin dig a deep hole. Mary brought a watering can.

Ben Weatherstaff brought a rose from the greenhouse. He knelt down by the hole and handed the plant to Colin. "Set it in the earth thyself, like the King does when he goes to a new place," he said.

Colin set the rose in the hole. Ben Weatherstaff helped firm the earth around it. Soot flew down to watch. Nut and Shell chattered from a cherry tree. When the rose was planted, Dickon helped Colin stand back up.

Colin stood straight and tall as the sun's last rays slipped behind the garden wall. He watched the sun slip away, laughing.

"It's Magic!" he said.

CHAPTER TWELVE

Magic

Dr. Craven was waiting in Colin's room when they went back inside.

"You should not have stayed outside so long," Dr. Craven told him.

"I am not tired at all," said Colin grandly. "It has made me better. Tomorrow I will stay outside all day. Don't you dare try to stop me!"

After Dr. Craven left, Mary sat and looked at Colin with a strange look on her face.

"What's wrong?" Colin wanted to know.

"I am thinking that I feel sorry for Dr. Craven," Mary said. "He has taken care of you for ten years and you are always rude to him.

Nobody dares to tell you how rude and spoiled you are, because you've always been so sick."

"Well, I am not going to be like that anymore," Colin said. "I stood on my feet this afternoon. I am getting well. If I go to the garden every day, I will stop being so spoiled. There is Magic there, Mary. I am sure of it."

In the months that followed, there was plenty of Magic in the garden. At first, green things pushed their way up through the earth. Then the green things opened into blue and purple and crimson flowers. The seeds Dickon and Mary planted grew as if fairies tended them. And the roses climbed the walls and spread over everything. First there were little green leaves, then the rose buds appeared. As the buds opened into flowers, they filled the garden with sweet scents.

Every day, Mary and Dickon pushed Colin in his wheelchair into the garden. He watched everything—the ants, beetles, bees, frogs, birds, flowers, shrubs, and trees. There was no end of things to look at and things to talk about or think over.

One day, Mary told Colin how she had wished

for him to stand up that first day in the garden. "I said, 'He can do it! He can do it!' over and over to myself," she told him. Colin was delighted—Mary had made a sort of Magic to help him.

The next morning, Colin called them all together—Mary, Dickon, and Ben Weatherstaff.

"Good morning," he said. "I want you to listen to me. When I grow up, I am going to be a great scientist. Right now, I am going to try a scientific experiment. Magic is all around us in this garden. I know it. This garden has made me well. When I stood that first time, Mary kept saying to herself, 'He can do it!' and I did. Of course, I had to try, but the Magic helped. Every day I am going to say, 'Magic is making me well!' That is my experiment. Will you help me?"

The children and Ben Weatherstaff all sat down in a circle under a tree. The crow, the fox, the squirrels, and the lamb slowly drew near and joined them. It was very quiet.

Colin thought it was good that the animals wanted to help, too. He started to chant, "The sun is shining! The flowers are growing! Being alive is Magic! Being strong is Magic! Magic is making me well!"

He said it many times. "Now I am going to walk round the garden," he said.

Colin led, with Mary and Dickon on either side. Sometimes Colin leaned on Dickon's arm, but only for a minute. Ben Weatherstaff followed and the creatures trailed behind him. Colin held his head high and looked very grand.

They stopped to rest. Colin said, "I want you to keep another secret. Don't tell anyone that I can walk yet. I want to be able to run. I want to surprise my father when he comes home. He will see that I am not sick anymore. He will be proud of me. I will be like other boys, and I will live to be a man."

Colin truly believed, now, that he was getting well. It made him happy to think of his father, and how he would look when he saw his son walking.

Soon after that, the nurse noticed how much Colin was eating at every meal. Walking and playing outside every day had made him hungry and put red in his cheeks.

"Your appetite is much better, Master Colin," she said. "You used to eat nothing."

"It's the fresh air," Colin told her. Then he worried that she would figure out his secret.

"Maybe I'm hungry because I have a strange new sickness."

"Perhaps," said the nurse, "but I must talk to Dr. Craven about it."

When Dr. Craven came, he asked a lot of questions. He was surprised at how well Colin looked.

"You stay out in the garden a great deal," he said. "Where do you go?"

"I won't tell anyone where I go," Colin answered. "You know I hate to be stared at."

"Well, being outside hasn't done you any harm," said the doctor. "The nurse says that you eat more than ever. You look much better. Your father will be happy to hear this."

"Do not tell him!" Colin shouted. "Do not write to my father!" Colin wanted to surprise his father himself. "I could get worse again any time, then he would be so disappointed!" Colin's face looked very angry, and he started to cry.

"Hush, my boy," Dr. Craven said. "I won't write to your father."

Mary and Colin decided to pretend that he was still sick. That way, no one would write to Mr. Craven to tell him the secret. Colin did not want his father to come home until he could walk and run by himself. They decided that they would stop eating so much. Instead of cleaning their plates, they would send most of the food back to the kitchen.

Dickon told his mother about the play acting Mary and Colin were doing. He said that the game made Colin and Mary laugh out loud.

"The more they laugh the better!" said his mother. "Laughter is better than pills any day!" She knew that two children who played outside all day must be very hungry. From then on, she sent rolls and milk along with Dickon to help keep Mary and Colin full.

Each day, Colin grew stronger and could walk further. He and Mary ate all the food that Dickon's mother sent. They sent her money with Dickon to buy them more. Dickon helped them build a little stone oven in the woods near the garden. Every day, they roasted potatoes there and ate as many as they liked. Now they hardly touched their meals at the manor house. The nurse and the servants began to worry that the children were starving. The nurse called the doctor.

Dr. Craven had not seen Colin for two weeks.

For a boy who was sickly, he looked very healthy. His skin was rosy and his eyes were clear. Dr. Craven didn't know what to do. When he talked to Mrs. Medlock on the way out, he said, "Going without food seems to agree with him. The boy looks better than ever."

"So does the girl," she said. "She's lost her sour look. You should hear them laugh! Perhaps they're getting fat on laughter."

"Then," said Dr. Craven, "let them laugh!"

CHAPTER THIRTEEN

The Curtain

There were Eggs in the robins' nest. Having the children near their nest made the robins nervous. The robin was not afraid of Dickon, though. Dickon could speak robin and move like a robin. He knew Dickon was a robin without beak or feathers. But Colin was another matter.

The robin watched Colin very carefully. He came into the garden in a thing with wheels. He walked about strangely. He was not at all steady on his feet at first. The others had to help him. He would walk a little, then stop to rest. His slow walk reminded the robin of cats waiting to pounce.

But then the robin remembered how he himself had learned to fly. He had taken short flights like this boy did. Then he had to rest, just like the boy. He told his mate that the Eggs would do the same when they learned to fly. They would stop and start, just like the boy did. She watched the boy. The Eggs, she said, would learn much more quickly. Humans were clumsier than Eggs. They never really learned to fly at all. You never met them in the air or up in the trees.

What really confused the robins was when the children did their exercises. Dickon had learned some exercises from a wrestler in the village. Dickon taught them to Colin to help him grow stronger. Mary did them, too. The robin could not understand why the children flapped their arms and legs around. It wasn't walking, or running, or flying. The robin was sure the Eggs would never flap about like that. It must be safe, though, because the boy who spoke robin did it.

One rainy morning, Mary and Colin were stuck inside. Colin was very restless. He had to stay in bed or on his couch so that the nurse wouldn't realize he could now walk.

"I wish it wasn't raining today. I wish my father would come home," he said. "Now that I am a real boy, I can't stand lying still like this. We can't pretend much longer."

Then Mary had a great idea. "Colin," Mary said. "We could explore the house! There are about a hundred rooms that no one ever goes into. There are long halls where you could run. We could even do our exercises. I went exploring when I first got here. One of the rooms I went into had a cabinet full of ivory elephants."

"Ring the bell," said Colin. When the nurse came in, he said, "I want my chair. Miss Mary and I will go alone to look at the closed-up part of the house. No one is to disturb us."

Off they went, with Colin in his chair. Rainy days would never be the same again. Colin and Mary explored. They ran and jumped and played, and did their exercises. They found the room with the ivory elephants and played with them. The children had a grand time.

At lunchtime, they went back to Colin's room. Mary noticed something. The curtain covering the picture of Colin's mother was open. She was surprised, and asked him about it.

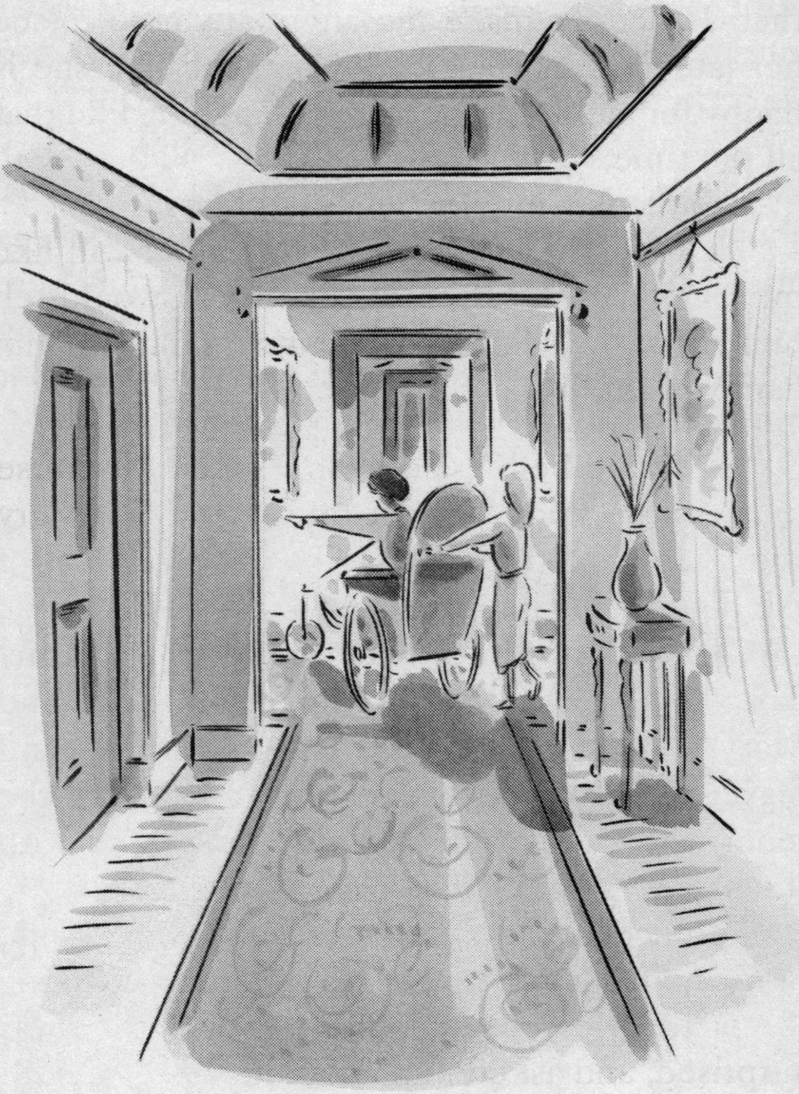

Colin told her, "I am going to keep it like that. It doesn't make me angry anymore to see her laughing. She looks down at me like she is happy for me. I want to see her laughing like that all the time."

"You look a lot like her," said Mary.

"If I look like her, maybe my father will like me," Colin said. "If he *did* like me, I would tell him about the Magic. Maybe it would make him happy again."

CHAPTER FOURTEEN

In the Garden

Every day the children had their Magic circle. Every day they did their exercises. They ran and played and laughed in the garden. And every day Colin grew stronger and straighter and healthier.

"Mary! Dickon!" he cried. "Just look at me! I'm well! I shall live forever and ever! I want to find out about everything that grows. I feel so happy! I want to shout out something thankful, joyful! I just want to sing, I feel so good!"

"Tha' might sing the Doxology," Ben Weatherstaff grunted.

"What is that?" Colin asked.

"Dickon can sing it for thee, I'll bet,"

Weatherstaff replied. "It's a song from church."

"Please sing it, Dickon," Colin said.

Dickon took off his cap. He said, "Ben, tha' must take off thy hat. You, too, Colin."

Then Dickon sang in a nice strong voice:

"Praise God from Whom all blessings flow,
Praise Him, all creatures here below,
Praise Him above, ye Heavenly Host,
Praise Father, Son, and Holy Ghost. Amen."

"It is a very nice song," Colin said. "It means just what I mean, that I am thankful. Please sing it again, Dickon. I want to sing it, too. How does it begin?"

Dickon sang it again, and Mary and Colin joined in. On the third time, Ben Weatherstaff sang, too. Mary saw that he had tears on his cheeks.

Just when they finished singing, Colin looked across the garden, startled.

"Who is coming in here?" he said quickly.

A woman was coming through the door. She had a long blue cloak and a nice smile. Dickon's eyes lit up.

"It's Mother!" he cried. "I told her where the door was."

Colin held out his hand to her shyly. "I've wanted to meet you," he said. "Are you surprised because I am so well?"

"Yes, I am!" Mrs. Sowerby said. "Tha' looks so much like thy mother, it surprises me. It made my heart jump a little when I saw thee."

"Do you think," said Colin, a little awkwardly, "that my father will like me?"

"Oh, yes, dear lad," she answered. "Thy father cannot help but like thee."

Dickon's mother had a basket filled with good things to eat. They all sat under a tree and talked and laughed and ate. Even Ben Weatherstaff had a good time.

"Can tha' believe it?" Ben asked Mrs. Sowerby. "The lad is as strong and as straight as any boy on the moor!"

"Aye, that he is," she answered. "It's just a miracle!"

Then she turned to Mary. "Tha' art grown fine and healthy, too. I'll bet tha' art like thy mother in looks. Tha' will look like a rose when tha' grows up, little lass."

They showed Dickon's mother their garden and told her the whole story. Colin walked on one

side of her and Mary on the other. They kept looking up at her, feeling warm and comfortable. They told her how the Magic had helped Colin get well.

"Aye," she said, "tha' art right about that. I heard thee singing of it. Call it whatever tha' likes, but never stop believing in it."

Mrs. Sowerby was full of fun and made them laugh. She laughed when they told her about pretending that Colin was still sick, so no one

would write to Mr. Craven.

"Tha' won't have to pretend much longer," she said. "Thy father will surely come home soon."

"Do you think he will?" asked Colin eagerly. "I think about it every day. I just want to run into his room."

"That would surely surprise him," said Dickon's mother. "I'd like to see his face. He would be shocked, but it would be such a good shock. He must come soon! He must!"

When it was time to leave, Colin stood very close to Dickon's mother. "I wish you were my mother, as well as Dickon's!" he said.

She hugged him close. "Dear lad!" she said. "Thy own mother's in this very garden, I do believe. She couldn't stay away from thee. And thy father will come back soon, too!"

❧

All that summer, Mr. Craven had wandered alone in faraway countries. No matter where he went, he did not see the beauty around him. He was a deeply sad and lonely man. One night, he walked along a lake. He walked so far that he got very tired.

He lay down on the ground and fell asleep. He dreamed that a sweet voice was calling him.

"Archie! Archie!" the voice called, and then, "In the garden! In the garden!"

He woke up calling his wife's name. He was sure that it had been her voice in the dream. "In the garden!" he said, wondering. "But the door is locked and the key is buried deep."

That day, he received a letter from Dickon's mother. It read:

Dear Sir,
Please, sir, come home. I think you would be glad to come. I think Mrs. Craven would ask you to come if she was here.
With my respects, Susan Sowerby

"I will go back to Misselthwaite," he said. "I'll go at once."

On his long journey home, he thought about his boy. For ten years, he had tried to forget him. He remembered how sad he was when Colin's mother died. He did not mean to be a bad father. He had given Colin the best doctors and bought him everything. But he could not be a real father to him. When he looked at the boy's eyes, he saw his wife and could only think about what he had lost. Now he began to think in a new way.

"Ten years is a long time," he thought. "Is it too late to do him good? Can I learn to be a better father to him?"

He decided to try to find the key to the garden. He didn't know why the garden was important, but he believed in his dream. When he arrived at Misselthwaite Manor, he sent for Mrs. Medlock.

"How is Master Colin, Medlock?" he asked.

"Well, sir," she answered slowly, "he's different. Not worse, but different. He eats a lot now, but he did not before. And he wants to be outside all the time. He used to be afraid to go out, but now he goes out every day with Mary and Dickon. They are in the garden right now."

"In the garden," he repeated. "*In the garden!*"

Mr. Craven walked outside and went slowly toward the secret garden. He knew where the door was, but he would have to look for the key. When he came to the door, he stopped and listened. He heard running and whispering inside the garden. There was quiet laughter. What in Heaven's name could it be?

The laughter grew closer. The feet ran faster and faster. The door flew open, and a boy ran out at full speed.

Mr. Craven gasped. The boy was tall and handsome. He looked at Mr. Craven with laughing eyes.

"Who? What? Who?" Mr. Craven stuttered.

This was not what Colin had planned. And yet, to come running out, winning a race, was even better. He stood tall.

"Father," he said, "I'm Colin."

Colin did not understand when his father said, "In the garden! In the garden!"

"Yes," Colin told him. "It was the garden that did it, and Mary and Dickon and the creatures, and the Magic. I'm well! Aren't you glad, Father? I'm going to live forever and ever and ever!"

Mr. Craven's soul shook with joy and he could not speak. Then he took Colin's hand. "Take me into the garden, my boy," he said at last, "and tell me all about it."

Colin led him into the garden. It was the beginning of fall. The sunshine was warm on the roses and the yellowing trees. There were fall flowers in gold and purple and scarlet on every side.

Mr. Craven stood there for a moment looking all around. "I thought it would be dead."

"Mary thought so at first, but then it came alive," Colin told him.

Then Colin told him the whole story—of the garden, and pretending, and of the Magic, and everything coming to life. Mr. Craven laughed until he cried. He was so happy that he cried, even when he was not laughing.

"And now, I will walk back with you, Father—to the house," said the healthy, rosy, happy boy to his smiling, loving father.

Ben Weatherstaff was in the kitchen with Mrs. Medlock. He had seen from his ladder in the next garden that the boy had met his father. Now Ben wanted to see the look on Mrs. Medlock's face when Colin came walking back to the house. He waved toward the window.

"Look there," he said. "Look who's coming."

When Mrs. Medlock looked, she gave a shriek. Everyone in the kitchen ran to the window and stared. Mr. Craven was coming. He looked happier than they had ever seen him. And by his side, with his head up, and eyes laughing, walked Master Colin.

THE END

FRANCES HODGSON BURNETT

Frances Hodgson was born in Manchester, England, in 1849. Like the characters in her stories, Mary Lennox from *The Secret Garden* and Sara Crewe from *A Little Princess*, Frances lost her father when she was very young. His death was very hard on the family, and they became quite poor. They left England when Frances was 16 years old, moving to an uncle's small farm near Knoxville, Tennessee.

Frances knew early in her life that she wanted to be a writer. She began publishing stories in magazines while still in her teens. These sales helped support her family. In 1873, she married Dr. Swan Burnett and lived in Washington, DC, and then in England. They had two sons, Lionel and Vivian.

Frances Hodgson Burnett wrote many plays and more than 40 novels for adults. Her most famous and beloved books, however, were three that she wrote for children—*Little Lord Fauntleroy* (1886), *A Little Princess* (1905), and *The Secret Garden* (1911).

Burnett became an American citizen, but still traveled and lived at times in England. She spent her later years in New York, and died in 1924.